Doctor De Soto, the dentist, did very good work, so he had no end of patients. Those close to his own size—moles, chipmunks, et cetera—sat in the regular dentist's chair.

Larger animals sat on the floor, while Doctor De Soto stood on a ladder.

For extra-large animals, he had a special room. There Doctor De Soto was hoisted up to the patient's mouth by his assistant, who also happened to be his wife.

Doctor De Soto was especially popular with the big animals. He was able to work inside their mouths, wearing rubbers to keep his feet dry; and his fingers were so delicate, and his drill so dainty, they could hardly feel any pain.

Being a mouse, he refused to treat animals dangerous to mice, and it said so on his sign. When the doorbell rang, he and his wife would look out the window. They wouldn't admit even the most timid-looking cat.

One day, when they looked out, they saw a well-dressed fox with a flannel bandage around his jaw.

"I cannot treat you, sir!" Doctor De Soto shouted. "Sir! Haven't you read my sign?"

"Please!" the fox wailed. "Have mercy, I'm suffering!" And he wept so bitterly it was pitiful to see.

"Just a moment," said Doctor De Soto. "That poor fox," he whispered to his wife. "What shall we do?"

"Let's risk it," said Mrs. De Soto. She pressed the buzzer and let the fox in.

He was up the stairs in a flash. "Bless your little hearts," he cried, falling to his knees. "I beg you, *do* something! My tooth is killing me."

"Sit on the floor, sir," said Doctor De Soto, "and remove the bandage, please."

Doctor De Soto climbed up the ladder and bravely entered the fox's mouth. "Ooo-wow!" he gasped. The fox had a rotten bicuspid and unusually bad breath.

"This tooth will have to come out," Doctor De Soto announced. "But we can make you a new one."

"Just stop the pain," whimpered the fox, wiping some tears away. Despite his misery, he realized he had a tasty little morsel in his mouth, and his jaw began to quiver. "Keep open!" yelled Doctor De Soto. "Wide open!" yelled his wife.

"I'm giving you gas now," said Doctor De Soto. "You won't feel a thing when I yank that tooth."

Soon the fox was in dreamland. "M-m-m, yummy," he mumbled. "How I love them raw...with just a pinch of salt, and a...dry... white wine."

They could guess what he was dreaming about. Mrs. De Soto handed her husband a pole to keep the fox's mouth open.

Doctor De Soto fastened his extractor to the bad tooth. Then he and his wife began turning the winch. Finally, with a sucking sound, the tooth popped out and hung swaying in the air.

"I'm bleeding!" the fox yelped when he came to.

Doctor De Soto ran up the ladder and stuffed some gauze in the hole. "The worst is over," he said. "I'll have your new tooth ready tomorrow. Be here at eleven sharp."

The fox, still woozy, said goodbye and left. On his way home, he wondered if it would be shabby of him to eat the De Sotos when the job was done.

After office hours, Mrs. De Soto molded a tooth of pure gold and polished it. "Raw with salt, indeed," muttered Doctor De Soto. "How foolish to trust a fox!"

"He didn't know what he was saying," said Mrs. De Soto. "Why should he harm us? We're helping him."

"Because he's a fox!" said Doctor De Soto. "They're wicked, wicked creatures."

That night the De Sotos lay awake worrying. "Should we let him in tomorrow?" Mrs. De Soto wondered.

"Once I start a job," said the dentist firmly, "I finish it. My father was the same way."

"But we must do something to protect ourselves," said his wife. They talked and talked until they formed a plan. "I think it will work," said Doctor De Soto. A minute later he was snoring.

The next morning, promptly at eleven, a very cheerful fox turned up. He was feeling not a particle of pain.

When Doctor De Soto got into his mouth, he snapped it shut for a moment, then opened wide and laughed. "Just a joke!" he chortled.

"Be serious," said the dentist sharply. "We have work to do." His wife was lugging the heavy tooth up the ladder.

"Oh, I love it!" exclaimed the fox. "It's just beautiful."

Doctor De Soto set the gold tooth in its socket and hooked it up to the teeth on both sides.

The fox caressed the new tooth with his tongue. "My, it feels good," he thought. "I really shouldn't eat them. On the other hand, how can I resist?"

"We're not finished," said Doctor De Soto, holding up a large jug. "I have here a remarkable preparation developed only recently by my wife and me. With just one application, you can be rid of toothaches forever. How would you like to be the first one to receive this unique treatment?"

"I certainly would!" the fox declared. "I'd be honored." He hated any kind of personal pain.

"You will never have to see us again," said Doctor De Soto.

"*No one* will see you again," said the fox to himself. He had definitely made up his mind to eat them—with the help of his brand-new tooth.

Doctor De Soto stepped into the fox's mouth with a bucket of secret formula and proceeded to paint each tooth. He hummed as he worked. Mrs. De Soto stood by on the ladder, pointing out spots he had missed. The fox looked very happy.

When the dentist was done, he stepped out. "Now close your jaws tight," he said, "and keep them closed for a full minute." The fox did as he was told. Then he tried to open his mouth—but his teeth were stuck together!

"Ah, excuse me, I should have mentioned," said Doctor De Soto, "you won't be able to open your mouth for a day or two. The secret formula must first permeate the dentine. But don't worry. No pain ever again!"

The fox was stunned. He stared at Doctor De Soto, then at his wife. They smiled, and waited. All he could do was say, "Frank oo berry mush" through his clenched teeth, and get up and leave. He tried to do so with dignity.

Then he stumbled down the stairs in a daze.

Doctor De Soto and his assistant had outfoxed the fox. They kissed each other and took the rest of the day off.